Elefantina's

Dream

Verse by **X. J. Kennedy**

Pictures by **Graham Percy**

Philomel Books

Elefantina's Dream

Watching ice-skaters skim
round the jumpy and dim
   tiny screen of her old TV,
Elefantina sighs
and with stars in her eyes
   cries, "If only that could be ME!

"Oh, how happy I'd feel
wearing blades of steel
   on a glimmery, glittery rink!
In my silvery suit
I could execute
   double cartwheels in a wink!

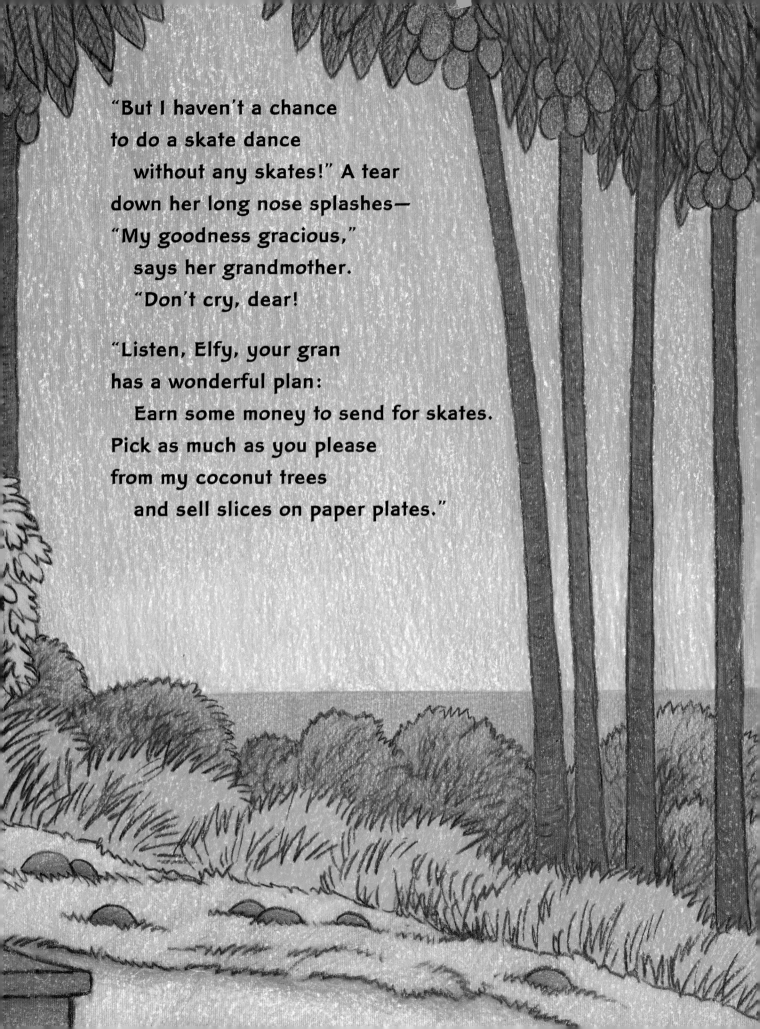

"But I haven't a chance
to do a skate dance
    without any skates!" A tear
down her long nose splashes—
"My goodness gracious,"
    says her grandmother.
    "Don't cry, dear!

"Listen, Elfy, your gran
has a wonderful plan:
    Earn some money to send for skates.
Pick as much as you please
from my coconut trees
    and sell slices on paper plates."

Soon ELFY'S NUT HUT
serving freshly-cut
    fast food is a hit. But where
will she skate in a town
where the sun beats down,
    making ice most exceedingly rare?

Oh, it never does freeze
in the coconut trees.
 Says Elfy, "Say, what if I
ask Tuskins the ice man—
he's a mighty nice man—
 to lend me his ice supply!"

In a big wide-floored
house where ice is stored
   for the chilling of lemonade,
wearing warm wool socks,
over huge blue blocks
   Elfy glides on her bright new blades.

From the dawn's first light
until late at night,
   hardly stopping to eat or drink,
her mind all afire
with her one desire,
   Elfy circles her makeshift rink.

Well, the days speed past—
Elfy's learning fast,
    and there in that ice-cold house
meets a whiskery soul
who lives in a hole—
    friendly Mozzarella Mouse.

Says the mouse, "Kid, you're *good*!
Hey, you really should
    try a super-spectacular jump.
Do a *salchow*—that's where
you turn in midair,
    and you land with a nice soft bump."

With encouragement from
her newfound chum,
    Elfy tries, but she clumsily trips,
and lands on her sitter,
but she's no quitter.
    She purses determined lips.

"The Elympic team
is this kid's big dream,"
   Mouse declares. "I'll phone today
and I'll ask, How about
letting Elfy try out?"
   "Send her in," says the team coach.
   HOORAY!

And with Mouse at her side,
Elfy's ready to ride,
   packs her skates and a box lunch of grain.
Hugging dear Gran tight
and promising she'll write,
   off she goes on the rattletrap train.

In the city next day,
breakfast hay put away,
　　she reports to the rink for her test,
where skaters who dream
of making the team
　　have assembled to skate their best.

All the candidates
lace up their skates
　　and the team coach, gruff and tough,
shifts his bubblegum quid
and tells Elfy, "Kid,
　　get out there and do your stuff."

Ah, to do her thing
makes her whole heart sing
　　and her hopes like a rainbow rise
(though since her arrival,
a dangerous rival
　　has watched her with jealous eyes).

Elfy's every minute
has skating in it:
    When she eats, when she falls into bed,
when she wakes with the sun
for a five-mile run,
    only skating is in her head.

Down the slithery ice
she can rapidly slice
    and over a barrel soar.
She can do swift swoops,
jumps, figures, and loops.
    "But," says Coach,
    "you'll need one thing more.

"To make the team, learn
the midair turn—
      that's the salchow—and learn it right.
Your big test's approaching—
don't you need extra coaching?"
      "I'll coach her," says Mouse, "tonight."

Owls hoot, stars wink
through the windows of the rink
    when Elfy and Mouse start working
on her salchow jump,
but she tumbles—KER-PLUMP!
    (Who's that in the darkness lurking?)

With deep-down sighing,
Elfy keeps on trying
    that difficult stunt. Toes numb,
bottom stiff and sore,
in the dorm once more
    she laments to her true-blue chum,

"Oh, Mozzarella,
I'm no Cinderella—
    is mine an impossible dream?
Is this all a mistake?
Will I ever skate
    a salchow—and make the team?"

The big day in the lives
of the skaters arrives—
   which ones will the judges pick
for the team? With glee
Elfy's enemy
   lays plans for a sneaky trick.

Just as Elfy skates by,
Trickster on the sly
   flings a slimy banana skin
and our innocent kid
does a dizzying skid
   and goes into a corkscrew spin!

She's out of control,
doing rock-and-roll!
  As she turns around terribly fast,
Elfy leaps through the air!
All the judges stare—
  she's done a salchow at last!

Trickster lets out a howl—
"My plan's gone foul!"
  And quick as a duck can quack,
dropping useless peels,
she takes to her heels
  and is gone—will she ever come back?

Elfy's made the team!
All the judges beam.
  They are applauding her one and all.
But—zippety zoom—
with a deafening BOOM,
  she rockets right through a wall.

In a month Elfy's able
back again to hobble
   to the rink. With a joyful tear,
she parks her crutches
and gingerly touches
   skates to ice.
   How her teammates cheer!

Well, little by little,
though her legs feel brittle,
   Elfy starts to regain her skill,
does a figure eight,
loops and swoops, and great
   spiral spins with never a spill.

 But can Elfy climb
back to health in time
   and in only a week compete
with skaters from
all Elephantdom
   in the great Elympic meet?

At last it's Elympics day!
The great games begin! HOORAY!

The uproarious crowd
cheers long and loud
   for each skater. Coach Mouse squeaks,
"Kid, you'd better do more
than ever before,
   or you'll lose, sure as birds have beaks!"

It's our heroine's turn!
All the crowd's eyes burn
    down upon her—excitement ripples!

Elfy's heart wildly beats
and she leaps—spins—completes
not a SINGLE salchow—but two TRIPLES!

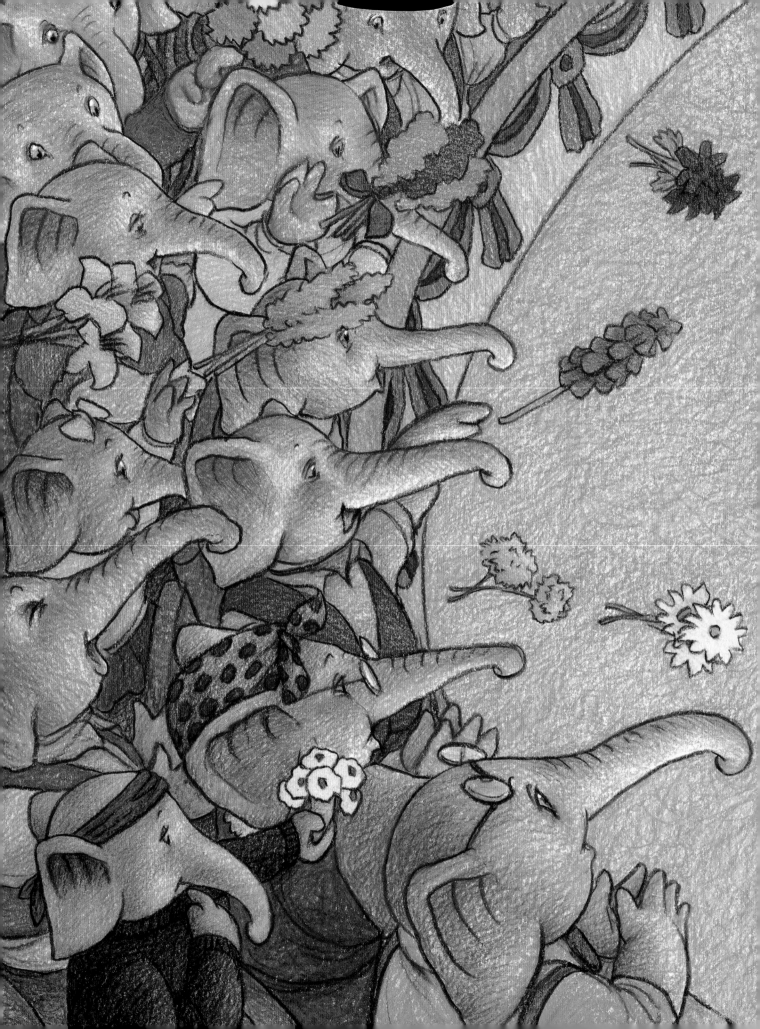

NOTES ON ICE SKATING

*F*igure skating has been a competitive sport for over 100 years. It was developed in the mid-1800s by Jackson Haines, an American ballet master who added elements of dance to skating. The first Olympic figure skating competitions were actually held during the Summer Olympics of 1908 and 1920—the Winter Olympics had not yet been created. When the first Winter Olympics were held in 1924, figure skating quickly became its most popular event. Gold medal-winning figure skaters throughout the years such as Sonja Henie, Peggy Fleming, Dorothy Hamill, Katarina Witt, and Tara Lipinski have been inspiring role models to young women of all nationalities.

The Olympic figure skating competition has four divisions: women's singles, men's singles, pairs, and ice dancing. In the singles competitions, skaters are judged in two events: a short program, which includes eight required elements (three jumps, three spins, and two fast footwork sequences), and a long program of free skating.

One of the most impressive elements to master is the salchow (pronounced "sow-cow") jump. The salchow is named after its originator, Ulrich Salchow, a Swedish skater who won the first-ever Olympic gold medal for men's figure skating. To do a salchow, a skater takes off from the edge of one foot, rotates in the air, and lands on the edge of the other foot. Depending on how many times the skater rotates, it may be classified as a single, double, triple, or even quadruple jump.

No elephant has ever been known to perform a triple salchow in competition.

For Caleb,
with mammoth fondness—X. J. K.

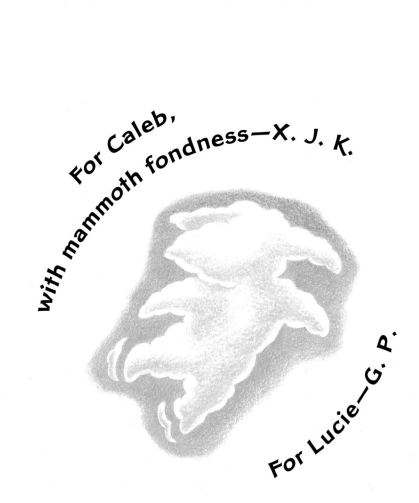

For Lucie—G. P.

Patricia Lee Gauch, editor

Text copyright © 2002 by X. J. Kennedy
Illustrations copyright © 2002 by Graham Percy
Philomel Books, a division of Penguin Putnam Books for Young Readers,
345 Hudson Street, New York, NY 10014.
Philomel Books, Reg. U.S. Pat. & Tm. Off. Published simultaneously in Canada.
Printed in Hong Kong by South China Printing Co. (1988) Ltd.

Book design by Sharon Murray Jacobs and Semadar Megged. The text is set in 16-point Clair Bold.
The art was created using crayons and colored pencils on Roberson cartridge paper.

Library of Congress Cataloging-in-Publication Data
Kennedy, X. J. Elefantina's dream / verse by X. J. Kennedy ; pictures by Graham Percy. p. cm.
Summary: With the help of Mozzarella Mouse, Elefantina the elephant trains hard to qualify for the Elympic ice-skating team.
[1. Ice-skating—Fiction. 2. Elephants—Fiction. 3. Stories in rhyme.] I. Percy, Graham, ill. II. Title.
PZ8.3.K384Ej 2002 [E]—dc21 00-036314 ISBN 0-399-23428-4
1 3 5 7 9 10 8 6 4 2
FIRST IMPRESSION